STEP INTO READING®

STEP 1

READY TO READ

THE EVIL PRINCESS
VS.
THE BRAVE KNIGHT
TAKE TURNS

by Jennifer L. Holm and Matthew Holm

Random House 🏠 New York

There is one
Evil Princess.

There is one
Brave Knight.

And there is one
big problem.
They both want
to go first.

Mwar?

But two people

cannot be first.

Their Magic Mirror
gives them a snack.

They both try

to choose first.

It does not work.

14

They both try to
get in first.

It does not work.

Take turns?

They do not like this.

The Evil Princess
does not like it.

Then they go to
the playground.

The Brave Knight
does not like it.

They return to
the castle.

Taking turns
is hard!

There is only
one cat to pet.

Maybe they can both
go first?

The Brave Knight
pets the cat's ears
first.

The Evil Princess

pets the cat's belly

first.

Everyone likes it.

Dear Parents:

Congratulations! Your child is taking the first steps on an exciting journey. The destination? Independent reading!

STEP INTO READING® will help your child get there. The program offers five steps to reading success. Each step includes fun stories and colorful art or photographs. In addition to original fiction and books with favorite characters, there are Step into Reading Non-Fiction Readers, Phonics Readers and Boxed Sets, Sticker Readers, and Comic Readers—a complete literacy program with something to interest every child.

Learning to Read, Step by Step!

Ready to Read   Preschool–Kindergarten
• big type and easy words • rhyme and rhythm • picture clues
For children who know the alphabet and are eager to begin reading.

Reading with Help   Preschool–Grade 1
• basic vocabulary • short sentences • simple stories
For children who recognize familiar words and sound out new words with help.

Reading on Your Own   Grades 1–3
• engaging characters • easy-to-follow plots • popular topics
For children who are ready to read on their own.

Reading Paragraphs   Grades 2–3
• challenging vocabulary • short paragraphs • exciting stories
For newly independent readers who read simple sentences with confidence.

Ready for Chapters   Grades 2–4
• chapters • longer paragraphs • full-color art
For children who want to take the plunge into chapter books but still like colorful pictures.

STEP INTO READING® is designed to give every child a successful reading experience. The grade levels are only guides; children will progress through the steps at their own speed, developing confidence in their reading. The F&P Text Level on the back cover serves as another tool to help you choose the right book for your child.

Remember, a lifetime love of reading starts with a single step!

For sweet Lily!

Visit us on the Web!
StepIntoReading.com
rhcbooks.com

Educators and librarians, for a variety of teaching tools, visit us at RHTeachersLibrarians.com

Library of Congress Cataloging-in-Publication Data
Names: Holm, Jennifer L., author. | Holm, Matthew, illustrator.
Title: The Evil Princess vs. the Brave Knight take turns / by Jennifer L. Holm and Matthew Holm.
Other titles: Evil Princess versus the Brave Knight take turns.
Description: New York : Random House Children's Books, [2020] | Series: Step into reading.
Level 1 | Audience: Ages 4–6. | Audience: Grades K–1. | Summary: "Siblings Evil Princess and Brave Knight learn to take turns." —Provided by publisher.
Identifiers: LCCN 2019038934 (print) | LCCN 2019038935 (ebook) |
ISBN 978-1-5247-7137-9 (trade paperback) | ISBN 978-1-5247-7138-6 (library binding) |
ISBN 978-1-5247-7139-3 (ebook)
Subjects: CYAC: Princesses—Fiction. | Knights and knighthood—Fiction. | Brothers and sisters—Fiction. | Behavior—Fiction. | Sharing—Fiction.
Classification: LCC PZ7.7.H65 Ew 2020 (print) | LCC PZ7.7.H65 (ebook) | DDC [E]—dc23

Printed in the United States of America

This book has been officially leveled by using the F&P Text Level™ Gradient Leveling System.

10 9 8 7 6 5 4 3 2 1